SPAN

Also in the Animal Ark Pets series

1 Puppy Puzzle
2 Kitten Crowd
3 Rabbit Race
4 Hamster Hotel
5 Mouse Magic
6 Chick Challenge
7 Pony Parade
8 Guinea-pig Gang
9 Gerbil Genius
10 Duckling Diary
11 Lamb Lessons
12 Doggy Dare
13 Donkey Derby
14 Hedgehog Home
15 Frog Friends
16 Bunny Bonanza
17 Ferret Fun
18 Rat Riddle
Cat Crazy
Pets' Party
Piglet Pranks
Foal Frolics

LUCY DANIELS

Spaniel Surprise

Illustrated by Paul Howard

A division of Hodder Headline Limited

Special thanks to Narinder Dhami

Created by Working Partners Limited, London W6 0QT
Original series created by Ben M. Baglio

First published in Great Britain in 2000
by Hodder Children's Books

3 5 7 9 10 8 6 4

A Catalogue record for this book is available from the British Library

ISBN 0 340 77878 4

Typeset by Avon Dataset Ltd, Bidford-on-Avon, Warks

Printed and bound in Great Britain by
The Guernsey Press Co. Ltd, Channel Isles

Hodder Children's Books
a division of Hodder Headline Limited
338 Euston Road
London NW1 3BH

Contents

1

Give a Dog a Home

"Quick, James! It's almost time!" Mandy Hope flew into the living-room and hurried over to the TV. Pushing her fair hair out of her eyes, she switched the TV on, then turned impatiently to see what had happened to her best friend, James Hunter. "*James!*"

"Sorry!" James hurried into the room a few

seconds later, carrying his Labrador pup, Blackie, in his arms. "Blackie spotted a spider, and was chasing it around the kitchen!"

"Bad boy, Blackie!" Mandy said, but she was smiling as she petted the puppy's sleek head. "Now, you *are* going to sit quietly and let us watch our favourite programme, aren't you?"

"Blackie never sits quietly – except when he's asleep!" James sighed, putting the puppy down. As if he'd heard what James said, Blackie immediately yawned widely, and went to curl

up on the rug in front of the Hopes' fire. Mandy and James looked at each other and laughed.

"Your dad's gone into the surgery to check on the overnight patients." Mandy's mother, Emily Hope, came in carrying a cup of coffee. "We've got quite a few, so he might be some time."

Mandy's parents were both vets, and their surgery, Animal Ark, was attached to the stone cottage where the family lived. Mandy was mad about animals, and knew most of the pets in the village of Welford, where she lived. She couldn't wait until she was twelve, when she would be allowed to help her parents in the surgery.

"Oh, is Dad going to miss *Give a Dog a Home*?" Mandy asked anxiously. "Shall we tape it for him?"

Mrs Hope nodded. "Good idea. I know he enjoys it."

"And then we can watch it again ourselves if we want to!" James pointed out.

Mandy grinned as she went over to the video

recorder to put a tape in. There were lots of animal programmes on TV and she and James watched most of them, but *Give a Dog a Home* was their absolute favourite. Each programme focused on a particular dog who needed a new owner, and viewers were invited to ring in and offer the dog a good home. The dogs were usually strays that were in poor condition, and often mistreated. Mandy and James were always thrilled to see the difference after the programme's "TLC Squad" had lavished lots of tender, loving care on them.

"Your father said he's going to pick up the Christmas tree tomorrow," Mrs Hope remarked, as she settled herself in a comfy armchair. "So you'll have to help me get the box of decorations down from the loft, Mandy."

"Oh, great!" Mandy exclaimed, as she put a blank video into the machine. It wasn't long now until Christmas. In fact, they only had two more days left at school before term ended.

"Quick, Mandy! It's starting!" James said, as the familiar theme tune began, accompanied by shots of some of the dogs who were housed in the *Give a Dog a Home* kennel near York. Mandy pressed "record" and hurried back to her seat on the sofa, next to James. They were doubly excited because tonight was the beginning of a new series. The programme had been off the air for the last few months, and Mandy and James had been longing for it to come back.

"Hello, and welcome to a new series of *Give a Dog a Home*!" The presenter, Fiona Ramsay, a young, red-haired woman in jeans and a leather jacket, was standing outside the kennel entrance, smiling into the camera. "We've got a packed programme for you tonight, including updates on the dogs who were rehomed in our last series."

The picture changed to show a fully grown Dalmatian trotting quietly along a street, a young, dark-haired man holding her lead.

"Oh, that's Tina, the dotty Dalmatian!" Mandy exclaimed in delight.

"Yes, do you remember how lively she was?" James said. "They were afraid her new owner might find her too much of a handful," James added. "But she looks OK, doesn't she?"

Mandy nodded, her eyes shining. She loved it when animals who had been written off were successfully rehomed.

"Later we'll be talking to dog psychologist Dr Richard Lacey about what you can do if your pet is becoming aggressive," Fiona Ramsay went on. "We'll also be weighing up the merits of dried dog food versus canned, and we'll be conducting some tests with the help of some of our canine friends from the *Give a Dog a Home* kennels! But first . . ."

The camera zoomed in closer as the presenter's smile faded, and she became more serious. "*Give a Dog a Home* is all about finding new homes for very special pups. And, with Christmas coming up, we all know about the problem of unwanted pets. But we have a very touching story for you tonight, about one little dog's search for a loving owner."

Mandy and James watched intently as Fiona Ramsay's face faded from the screen, and a picture of the kennel's reception area flashed up instead. The TLC squad, Lynn, Mel and Andy, were there. Lynn and Andy were taking calls on the phones, and Mel was at the computer. They were all dressed in their usual uniforms of jeans and bright-red sweatshirts, emblazoned with the words "TLC SQUAD – Give a Dog a Home"!

"Three months ago, the staff at the *Give a Dog a Home* kennel received an urgent call," the voiceover by Fiona Ramsay explained. "A local woman had found a young terrier lying

at the roadside, obviously injured and distressed. The TLC squad got on the case immediately."

The film switched to a shot of the TLC Squad jumping into their distinctive red van, and driving to the terrier's aid. Mandy and James exchanged looks of horror as the van stopped, and the camera zoomed in on the little dog lying in the gutter.

"Oh no!" Mandy gasped. The dog's reddish-brown, wiry coat was matted and bloodstained, and one of his back legs was hanging in a very awkward position. He was also very, very thin. His eyes were closed, and he was whimpering faintly.

"It looks like this poor little fellow has been hit by a car," Mel announced solemnly, after she'd done a quick examination of the terrier. "His leg might be broken, but our vet will have to check that out."

"It's possible that he's a stray," Lynn went on, as she gently stroked the dog's head with one finger, "because he's in very poor condition. But it's also possible that he was abandoned here, maybe even thrown out of a car by his original owner, and that's how he got injured."

"How can people be so cruel?" Mandy sat bolt upright, her face pale with anger and her fists clenched.

"I know," James agreed sadly. "But at least we know he must be OK, if he's going to be rehomed."

"That's true," Mrs Hope said gently.

The TLC squad had taken the terrier back to the kennel, where he was seen immediately by the *Give a Dog a Home* vet. The news was a mixture of good and bad. The dog's leg was broken, but it was a clean break, and the vet thought it would heal well. He was more worried by the fact that the little terrier was in very poor condition, and seemed half-starved.

"It's going to take a lot of tender, loving care to nurse this poor little pup back to health," Andy said, as the vet prepared to treat the dog's broken leg. "But that's what the TLC squad is here for!"

"And we've decided to call him Rusty, because of the colour of his coat," Mel added.

"Check back with us later in the programme to see how Rusty gets on!" Lynn finished off.

"Rusty! That's a lovely name," Mandy said, as the programme began showing the interview with Dr Richard Lacey, the dog psychologist.

"I bet lots of people are going to ring in and offer Rusty a good home!" James said eagerly.

Mandy and James always enjoyed the rest of *Give a Dog a Home*, with its mixture of interviews and interesting information about dogs, but tonight they were particularly impatient to find out what had happened to Rusty. They had to wait until about ten minutes before the end of the programme before he was mentioned again.

"And now, back to our featured dog." Fiona Ramsay smiled into the camera. "I'm sure you're all longing to know how Rusty's got on over the last three months—"

"We are!" Mandy said, bouncing impatiently up and down on the sofa.

"Well, let's take a look, shall we?" The presenter looked round, and called "Rusty!"

Two seconds later a little terrier was racing towards her, barking, his tail wagging madly from side to side. His coat was as shiny as if it had been polished, and he looked the picture of health. Beaming, Fiona Ramsay bent down so that Rusty could jump into her arms. He snuggled down happily, trying to lick the presenter's nose.

"Yes, this *is* Rusty!" Fiona Ramsay laughed. "I bet you can't believe your eyes!"

"I can't!" James pushed his glasses up his nose, and stared at the TV. "He ought to be called Shiny now, not Rusty! Doesn't he look great, Mandy?"

"Yes, he does." Mandy had a big lump in her throat. It was almost impossible to believe that it was the same dog. She couldn't help hoping that Rusty's former owners were watching. Then they would see what a difference a bit of loving care could make to a dog's life.

There was an interview with the vet, who confirmed that Rusty had made a full recovery, and then an interview with the TLC squad, accompanied by shots of Rusty being taken for a walk.

"Rusty's a great dog, full of life!" Mel said, smiling. "And he's very good with children."

"He can be noisy and boisterous," Andy pointed out. "But he's responding well to basic training."

Mandy and James laughed and applauded as Rusty obeyed the commands of sitting, staying and coming to heel, without putting a foot wrong.

"Rusty would make a wonderful pet," Lynn went on. "He needs a lot of attention, but he'll pay you back by giving you lots of love!"

There was a close-up of Rusty's appealing face as he looked up at Fiona Ramsay, before the presenter turned to the camera again.

"So, would *you* like to offer Rusty a loving new home? If you would, here's the number to ring . . ."

"I bet they'll get lots of calls!" James exclaimed, as the theme tune and end credits began.

"Of course they will!" Mandy agreed

immediately. She smiled as the programme finished with more film of Rusty playing happily with the TLC squad. "Who wouldn't want a cute little dog like Rusty?"

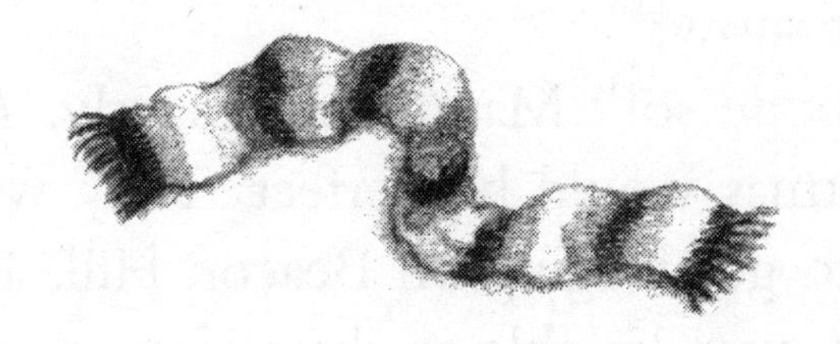

2

Holly and Mince Pies

"I wonder if Rusty's found a new owner yet," James said, as he and Mandy walked through the village to school the following morning.

"I think it probably takes quite a while," Mandy pointed out. "The *Give a Dog a Home* kennel will want to check people out carefully, to make sure Rusty gets just the right home."

"Yes, I suppose so." James shivered, and tucked his long stripy scarf more firmly into his coat. "It's cold, isn't it? Do you think it might snow?"

"I hope so!" Mandy said eagerly. A white Christmas would be perfect. They would be able to go sledging on Beacon Hill, and they might even be able to skate if the pool at the bottom of the hill froze solid.

"I hope Rusty gets his new home in time for Christmas!" James said, looking pleased. "Wouldn't that be great?"

"Hello, Mandy! Hello, James!"

Mandy and James turned round to see Libby Masters and her friend Ben Hardwick, both muffled up in woolly hats and scarfs, their noses red from the cold. They were a few years younger than Mandy and James, but they all knew each other well.

"Hi, Libby, hi Ben!" Mandy grinned. "How's Ryan, Libby?"

Libby's face lit up. She loved talking about her baby brother. "He's great!" she said enthusiastically.

Mandy smiled. She could remember a time when Libby hadn't been too happy at the thought of having a baby brother or sister, so it was nice to see how much she loved Ryan now.

"Did you see *Give a Dog a Home* last night?" Ben asked eagerly.

James nodded. "Yes, I watched it with Mandy. Wasn't Rusty brilliant?"

"Oh, he was great!" Ben said breathlessly. "I videoed the programme, and I watched it again this morning."

"Twice!" Libby said teasingly. "He was still watching it when I went round to call for him!"

"I'd love a dog like Rusty," Ben said wistfully.

Mandy glanced at James. They both knew that Ben was desperate for a dog, and had been for quite some time now. Mandy felt really sorry for him. She couldn't have a pet herself because her parents were so busy with the surgery, but at least she was always surrounded by animals at Animal Ark, even if they belonged to other people. But Ben didn't even have that.

"I wanted to ring up about giving Rusty a home," Ben went on sadly, as they all went into the school playground. "But Mum said no. She said terriers are too noisy."

"Well, most dogs can be noisy!" Mandy said carefully. "But you can always train them to be quiet!"

Ben nodded, still looking rather downcast. Libby took his arm. "Come on, let's go and join in with the rounders game."

"Poor Ben!" Mandy said, as the two younger

children ran off to join their classmates, who were playing rounders on the other side of the playground. "He wants a dog so badly."

"Do you remember what happened when the last series of *Give a Dog a Home* was on?" James asked. "Ben wanted to ring up about every single dog that was looking for a new owner!"

Mandy frowned. "Yes, and his mum always said no."

"That's right." James pushed his glasses higher up his nose. "She kept saying the dogs were too big, too small, too old, too noisy . . ."

"It sounds to me like Mrs Hardwick just doesn't like dogs much, and so she's making excuses," Mandy said thoughtfully.

Mandy and James looked at each other, and sighed. It certainly didn't look as if Ben was going to be Rusty's new owner. In fact, Ben's chances of getting a dog at all seemed very slim indeed.

"Only one more day to go!" James said with satisfaction, as he and Mandy joined the rush to escape from school at the end of the day. "I can't wait for the holidays!"

"Neither can I!" Mandy said enthusiastically. The day had been spent helping their teachers to clear up their classrooms, and put everything in order before the end of term. Mandy was relieved that they hadn't had to do any work, because she had been thinking about Ben all day, and wouldn't have been able to concentrate.

"I was wondering if there was anything we could do to help Ben," James said, as they left the school playground. "He's been on my mind all day."

Mandy nodded. "Me too!" Then she looked solemn. "Maybe I could ask Mum or Dad to talk to Mrs Hardwick about the kind of dog that would suit them. But Ben's mum might not like it."

James nodded. "Maybe she'll change her mind about Rusty anyway. After all, it *is* Christmas!"

"Oh, that reminds me," Mandy said suddenly, "I've got to call in on Gran and

Grandad. Gran's baked me some cakes for our class party tomorrow."

"I wish I was in *your* class!" James said enviously. He was a year younger than Mandy, and in the class below her. "I *love* your gran's cooking!"

Mandy grinned. "Don't worry, I'll save you some!" she promised as they made their way to Lilac Cottage.

Gran and Grandad were very busy with their preparations for Christmas. Grandad was arranging sprigs of holly on the mantelpiece, and Gran was hard at work in the kitchen. Lilac Cottage was full of the delicious smell of baking. And with the roaring fire, and twinkling fairy lights draped on the beautifully decorated tree in the corner, Mandy thought it all felt very Christmassy.

"Do you want some holly to decorate Animal Ark, Mandy?" Grandad asked, as he finished tucking the last sprig in place. "We've got plenty left. I managed to cut quite a bit this year before the birds ate all the berries!"

"That would be great, Grandad," Mandy said

with a grin. "But it's a shame for the poor old birds!"

"Don't worry," Grandad replied with a wink. "We've been putting out nuts for them for the last couple of weeks. I'll pop over tomorrow with the holly."

"I've made you some mince pies, a jam sponge and some little fairy cakes." Mandy's Gran bustled in from the kitchen, carrying some airtight tins. "Will that be enough?"

"Oh, brilliant, Gran. Thank you!" Mandy said gratefully.

"And here's a few mince pies for your class, James." Gran handed him a tin, too, and James's face lit up.

"Thanks very much, Mrs Hope!" he said.

"Now how about some mince pies and a cup of hot chocolate before you go?" Gran went on, and Mandy and James looked at each other in delight.

While they were eating, Mandy told her grandparents about Ben, and how much he wanted a dog.

"We saw *Give a Dog a Home* last night," Grandad said, sipping his chocolate. "That Rusty was a real character."

"Yes, he'd make a lovely pet," Gran agreed.

"I don't think Mrs Hardwick thinks so," Mandy sighed.

"You've got that look in your eyes again, Mandy!" Grandad teased her.

"What look?" Mandy wanted to know.

"The look that means you're going to try

and do something to help Ben!" Grandad smiled at her.

"If Mrs Hardwick doesn't like dogs, dear, there's not much you can do about it," Gran said, as she handed round the mince pies.

"Maybe Gran's right," Mandy said, as she and James left Lilac Cottage, feeling very warm inside, and full of mince pies. "Maybe Mrs Hardwick's *never* going to let Ben have a dog."

"You're giving up before you've even started!" James exclaimed. "That's not like you, Mandy!"

Mandy couldn't help smiling as they walked through the village. But, before she could say anything, something else caught her attention.

"Look, James!" she said, grabbing his arm. "Isn't that Ben?"

"Yes, it is!" James squinted through his glasses. "What *is* he doing?"

Ben was acting very strangely. He was wandering up and down the narrow street, stopping now and then to peer into every garden and alleyway. He was concentrating so hard on what he was doing that he didn't even notice Mandy and James.

"I don't know." Mandy frowned. "But I think we ought to find out. Come on!"

3

Poor Ben!

"Ben!" Mandy called, but she had to say his name twice before he heard her. "Ben, what on earth are you doing?"

Ben blushed a fiery red as he suddenly saw Mandy and James walking towards him.

"Nothing."

"Have you lost something?" James asked.

"If you have, we'll help you look," Mandy offered.

There was silence for a moment or two, as Ben shuffled his feet in embarrassment. "I was looking for a dog," he muttered at last.

"A dog!" Mandy exclaimed, surprised.

"Whose dog?" James asked.

"A stray dog." Ben bit his lip. "I just thought that if I could find a stray dog running about Mum would let me keep it."

Mandy glanced at James. Poor Ben must have been really desperate for a dog to spend ages out in the cold on the off-chance that he might find a stray pet. And, even if he did, would his mum have let him keep it?

"I don't think it's a good idea, Ben," Mandy said gently. "Even if you did find a dog, it might not be a stray at all, and then you'd have to give it back to its real owner."

Ben's face fell. "I hadn't thought of that."

"Haven't you been home yet?" Mandy asked, noting that Ben still had his schoolbag with him.

"No." Ben shook his head, as James glanced at his watch.

"It's getting pretty late," James pointed out. "Won't your mum be worried?"

Ben heaved a huge sigh. "Yes, I suppose I'd better get back."

"We'll walk you home," Mandy said, with a quick look at James to make sure he agreed. It was quite dark by now and, although Welford was a safe place to live, Mandy didn't think Ben's mum would like the idea of him wandering around looking for stray dogs. Anyway, it was an opportunity to talk to Mrs Hardwick.

"Ben!" As soon as they opened the gate to the Hardwicks' house, Ben's mum flung open the front door. "Where have you been? I was getting worried!"

Mandy didn't say anything, knowing it was up to Ben to tell his mum what he'd been doing.

"Sorry," Ben muttered sheepishly.

"Too busy playing football after school, I expect!" Mrs Hardwick said with a relieved smile. "Hello, Mandy. Hello, James. Thank you for walking Ben home. Would you like to come in for a drink and some biscuits?"

"Oh, yes please," Mandy said immediately. She wasn't hungry at all, but this was too good a chance to miss.

"I'll burst if I eat any more!" James whispered in her ear, as they followed Ben into the Hardwicks' living-room.

"I know, but it's all in a good cause!" Mandy whispered back.

Ben had hurried over to the TV, and was switching it on.

"Let's watch the *Give a Dog a Home* video," he said eagerly. "Just the bits about Rusty."

"Oh, Ben, not that programme again," Mrs Hardwick complained as she carried a tray of drinks and a plate of biscuits into the room. Ben was fast-forwarding to the part where Rusty was discovered injured by the roadside. "You've already watched it twice today!"

"But it's great, Mum!"

Mandy saw how intently Ben watched the programme, and how he couldn't take his eyes

off Rusty. She could also see the frown on Mrs Hardwick's face. Things didn't look good for Ben and his dream of owning a dog.

"This is my *favourite* bit!" Ben said happily, as the healthy, shiny-coated Rusty raced up and down with the TLC squad. They all watched right until the end when the telephone number for people who wanted to be the dog's new owner was given out, and then Ben turned to his mum. Mandy could guess what was coming next.

"Mum, can I ring the programme about Rusty? *Please!* There's still time!"

"Oh, Ben!" Mrs Hardwick looked very uncomfortable indeed. "We've already had this conversation. Dogs are more trouble than they're worth. And terriers are very noisy. Everyone knows that they're very yappy little dogs."

"But Rusty wouldn't be!" Ben said desperately. "I'd train him to be quiet."

"No, Ben!" said Mrs Hardwick, and there was such a sharp tone to her voice that Mandy was a bit surprised. "If you have a dog at all, it has to be the right one for *us*. We couldn't possibly have a noisy dog, so don't ask me about Rusty again, please."

Ben's face fell, but Mandy's ears had pricked up. It sounded like Mrs Hardwick might be willing to let Ben have a dog, if they could just find one that she didn't object to.

"Your mum's right, you know, Ben," Mandy said gently. "You have to make sure you choose the right dog for *you*."

"Exactly!" Mrs Hardwick agreed, sounding relieved. "After all, Ben, it would be awful if the dog didn't fit into our family and we had to get rid of it."

Mrs Hardwick's voice sounded a bit shaky as she said that. Mandy wondered why, but she didn't feel she could ask.

"So even if I can't have Rusty, can I choose *another* dog?" Ben asked eagerly.

"We'll see," Mrs Hardwick said vaguely. "We'll talk about it after Christmas."

Ben looked really disappointed, but he didn't say anything. Mandy and James said their goodbyes and went, leaving both Ben and Mrs

Hardwick looking rather glum.

"That sounded a bit more hopeful, didn't it?" James said, as they went through the gate.

Mandy sighed. "Well, Mrs Hardwick didn't exactly *say* that Ben could have a dog."

"No, I know," James agreed. "But if we can just find the right dog for Ben, then maybe she'll say yes!"

"Yes, maybe," Mandy replied. But she had a suspicion that Ben's mum was going to prove very hard to please . . .

When Mandy got back to Animal Ark, she popped into the surgery at the back of the house. The evening appointments had just started, and the waiting-room was already filling up with patients. Mandy said hello to Jean the receptionist, then she spotted Richard Tanner, who was in her class at school, patiently waiting his turn. He had his Persian cat, Duchess, in a basket on his lap. Duchess was crouched down in the basket looking miserable.

"Hi, Richard." Mandy bent down to take a

closer look at the cat. "What's wrong?"

"Duchess didn't eat anything today," Richard said glumly. "Then, when I got home from school, she looked so miserable, I thought I'd better bring her to Animal Ark."

"I hope she'll be OK for Christmas," Mandy said, poking her finger into the basket to try and stroke the white cat. But Duchess just stared listlessly at her.

"Richard?" Emily Hope opened the door to the consulting-room, looking very professional in her white coat. "I'll see Duchess now." She smiled as she spotted Mandy. "I think we're going to be flat out tonight, love! Every single appointment is booked!"

"Don't worry about me!" Mandy said cheerfully. She was used to Animal Ark taking up large amounts of her parents' time, and she didn't mind a bit. All that mattered was that sick animals got the help they needed to make a full recovery.

"Make yourself a sandwich if you get hungry," her mum told her, as she ushered an anxious Richard into the consulting-room.

"Oh, and your father picked up a Christmas tree today from Mr Fenton. So you can start decorating it if you like."

"Brilliant!" Mandy exclaimed. George Fenton owned a sawmill on the edge of the village, and at Christmas he sold trees at his workshop. The Hopes had bought their tree from him for as long as Mandy could remember – it had become a Christmas tradition.

Mandy wasn't hungry just yet, so she hurried into the living-room to take a look at the tree. As usual, it was the biggest one they could fit into the room, with just enough space for a silver star on top. Mandy grinned, and plunged her hands into the big box of decorations she and her mum had brought down from the loft the night before. Pulling out tinsel, glittering glass ornaments and silver baubles, she carefully began to decorate the tree, but her mind was only half on the job. She was still thinking about Ben and wondering if there was any way they could persuade Mrs Hardwick to agree once and for all that he could have a dog.

Then Mandy's face lit up. "Of course!" she

said to herself with a smile, as an idea began to form in her mind.

4

Taking Care of Blackie

"There's Ben!" Mandy nudged James, as they walked into the school playground. She couldn't wait to put her plan into action. She had told James about it on the way to school, and he thought it was a brilliant idea.

"He's looking pretty miserable," James

observed as they went over to him.

"Well, it's too late for him to ring up about Rusty now," Mandy sighed, waving to Richard Tanner, who looked much happier this morning. Mandy's mum had told her that Duchess had a viral infection, and that the cat would be fine after a course of pills. "But I'm sure there's another dog somewhere who'd be just perfect for Ben!"

"Don't forget Mrs Hardwick," James reminded her, and Mandy nodded. It was just as important to please Mrs Hardwick as it was to find the right dog for Ben. But it certainly wasn't going to be easy.

"Hi, Ben," Mandy said warmly, as they stopped in front of the younger boy.

"Hello," Ben muttered, and Mandy's heart went out to him. He certainly was miserable.

"Are you looking forward to your class party?" James asked.

"I suppose so," Ben sighed, but he didn't seem too enthusiastic. Mandy hoped that what she had planned would make him feel a whole lot better.

"What are you doing tomorrow, Ben?" she asked.

Ben blinked at the unexpected question. "I don't know," he said. "Why?"

"Well, James and I are planning to go for a walk along the local nature trail in the morning," Mandy explained. "You know, the one that starts near Beacon Hill? We were wondering if you wanted to come with us."

Ben looked a bit more cheerful. "OK, I'll have to ask my mum, though."

"Maybe your mum would like to come along too," Mandy suggested. It was, in fact, very important that Mrs Hardwick came with them if Mandy's plan was going to work. "We have to have a grown-up with us, you see."

"All right." Ben nodded. "Shall I ask Libby to come too?"

"Yes, why not?" Mandy agreed.

"I'll go and ask her now." Ben was looking a lot happier. "And if Mum can't come, maybe Libby's mum will."

Mandy glanced at James. That wouldn't

work at all! They'd just have to hope that Mrs Hardwick agreed.

"Are you bringing Blackie, James?" Ben asked eagerly.

"Of course I am!" James replied.

Ben's eyes lit up. "Oh, great!" he exclaimed, as he raced off to find Libby.

Mandy and James looked at each other and laughed.

"Let's hope it all goes to plan tomorrow!" Mandy said. If all did go well, there was a chance that Ben would have his dog in time for Christmas.

"You want *me* to take care of Blackie on the walk?"

Ben's face was a picture of excitement, as he stared at James and Mandy with wide eyes.

"Well, you want to learn how to look after a dog, don't you?" James laughed, holding out Blackie's lead. "Go on, take it!"

Mandy watched, smiling, as Ben took hold of Blackie's lead as carefully as if it was made of glass. The puppy was already snuffling around in the hedgerow at the start of the nature trail.

It was a bright, frosty morning, and the grass was crisp underfoot. All the trees were white with frost, and even the spiders' webs hanging in the bushes were coated in glistening silver. Mandy thought it all looked beautiful. She took a deep breath of the clean, cold air, and glanced at Mrs Hardwick. Luckily Ben's mum had agreed to come with them.

"Good dog, Blackie," Ben said happily, patting the puppy's head, and Blackie stopped exploring long enough to give the young boy's hand a friendly lick.

Mandy watched Mrs Hardwick staring at Ben and Blackie with a very strange look on her face, and wondered what she was thinking.

"We need to go that way," Libby Masters said. She was studying the signs ahead of them. The trail was marked out with pictures of a squirrel nibbling a nut, so there was no chance of them losing their way.

"How long is the trail?" James asked, as they set off.

"About two kilometres," Mandy replied.

James groaned. "I hope I can keep up!" he said. "I'm still full from our class party yesterday!"

"Well, you shouldn't have eaten so many of Gran's mince pies!" Mandy teased him.

"It's lucky that I'm looking after Blackie today, then," Ben called as the puppy trotted along in front of everyone else, pulling Ben with him. "You can have a rest, James."

"Thanks, Ben," James called back.

"Wait for me!" Libby shouted, running to catch her friend and Blackie up.

Mandy wasn't sure that they would see much wildlife on the trail. Animals such as squirrels would probably have begun hibernating now that the cold weather had arrived. But there were still birds foraging for food, and a robin was perched in the lower branches of a tree, watching them with its bright eyes.

Anyway, Ben and Blackie certainly seemed to be enjoying themselves. Mandy watched as Blackie stopped to investigate an interesting smell at the base of a tree trunk. Ben took the

opportunity to pet and stroke the puppy, and Blackie immediately lost interest in the scent and happily allowed Ben to fuss him. Ben turned to say something to Libby, which Mandy couldn't hear, but it was obvious from his shining eyes and happy smile that he was enjoying himself enormously. Mandy glanced at Mrs Hardwick. Even she was smiling as she watched her son having so much fun.

"Blackie's a Labrador puppy, isn't he?" Mrs Hardwick asked suddenly.

"Yes," James agreed, and Mandy felt a sudden surge of hope. Mrs Hardwick taking an interest in Blackie might be a very good sign.

Ben's mum frowned. "Labradors are big dogs when they're fully-grown, aren't they?" she remarked. "Doesn't your mother mind, James?"

Mandy's heart sank. Why did Mrs Hardwick only ever seem to see the *bad* things about dogs?

"No, she loves Blackie," James said quickly. "And we've got room to have a big dog, too." He glanced at Mandy and added, "A Labrador wouldn't suit *everybody*."

"But there are lots of different kinds of dogs." Mandy was quick to jump in at this point. "Just like there are lots of different kinds of people."

"Yes, but unfortunately Ben always seems to want the *wrong* kind of dog!" Mrs Hardwick said quietly, watching Ben laughing as Blackie eagerly pulled him along.

"What do you mean, the wrong kind of dog?" Mandy asked politely. Just as she had hoped, bringing Ben and Blackie together had brought up the subject of dogs – and now that the conversation had begun, Mandy was determined to find out exactly why Mrs Hardwick was so reluctant to let Ben have a pet.

"Well . . ." For a change, Mrs Hardwick looked rather unsure of herself. "Dogs are a lot of work, and Ben always seems to want dogs that are too big or too small, for a start. We haven't got a very large house, so a big dog is out of the question. And I'd be worried about a small dog getting under my feet all the time."

"Well, there are lots of medium-sized dogs," Mandy pointed out gently.

"And Ben's bound to want a puppy," Mrs Hardwick went on. "I just don't have time to look after a puppy."

"I think Ben just wants a dog." James backed Mandy up firmly. "I don't think he'd mind if it wasn't a puppy."

"There are plenty of adult dogs in the animal shelters," Mandy pointed out. "And the staff there can tell you if they're quiet or noisy or whatever you want to know." She took a deep breath. It was now or never. "If we could find a nice, quiet, fully grown dog for Ben, do you think he might be allowed to have it?"

"Blackie!" Ben was helpless with laughter and so was Libby. Blackie had nosed his way into a hole in the hedgerow, and had come out with his ears white with frost, which made him look as if he'd been iced like a wedding cake. The puppy gave his head a vigorous shake, and Ben bent down and hugged him.

"You're great, Blackie!" he said. "I wish I had a dog like you!"

Mandy looked at Ben's mum, still waiting for an answer. Mrs Hardwick was smiling, but she looked sad too.

"I suppose a quiet, gentle dog wouldn't be too much bother," Mrs Hardwick muttered, almost to herself. "As long as it wasn't a puppy . . ."

Mandy's eyes lit up, and she glanced at James. He was also looking thrilled.

"Do you mean Ben *can* have a dog, Mrs Hardwick?" Mandy asked breathlessly.

"Well . . ." Ben's mum still looked

undecided. But, as she glanced at Ben and Blackie again, her eyes softened. "All right. Ben can have a dog – but only if we can find the right one!"

5

Freddie

"Mum! Do you mean it? I really can have a dog?"

Ben's eyes were shining, and he was staring at his mother as if he could hardly believe what she'd just told him.

"Now, don't get too excited, dear," Mrs Hardwick said quickly.

They had just dropped Libby off at Blackheath Farm where the Masters lived, and were on their way back to Welford. Mandy had hardly been able to stop herself from telling Ben that his mum had finally agreed to his requests for a dog, but she'd managed to keep quiet and let Mrs Hardwick tell him herself. It had taken her quite a while to get round to it, though. Mandy hoped that didn't mean she was changing her mind again.

"That's fantastic!" Ben bounced up and down in his seat, a big grin on his face. "Thanks, Mum! You're the best mum in the whole world!"

Mandy could see that Mrs Hardwick was pleased, even though she tried to speak quite sternly.

"Now calm down, Ben. Dogs are a lot of work, and first you've got to promise to look after it. And, as I said before, any dog we adopt has to be the right one for us—"

Ben wasn't listening. "Can we go to the animal shelter now, Mum?" he demanded. "And can Mandy and James come too?"

Mrs Hardwick looked rather shocked. "What, right now?" she exclaimed. "But it's lunch-time. I'm sure Mandy and James have other plans for this afternoon."

"No, we haven't," Mandy and James said together. Mandy was secretly starting to get a bit worried that Mrs Hardwick might change her mind if she had more time to think about it. The sooner Ben found his dog, the better.

"I was thinking of waiting until after Christmas—" Mrs Hardwick began, but Ben interrupted her.

"But I don't want to wait!" he complained. "I want to go now! Then we'll have the dog in time for Christmas!"

"You might not be able to, Ben," Mandy said gently. "Lots of animal shelters won't rehome dogs and puppies close to Christmas-time. It's so that they're not given as presents." Ben's face fell, and Mandy went on quickly. "But you can choose a dog now, even if you can't take it home until *after* Christmas."

Ben immediately cheered up again. "That's what we'll do, then!" he said firmly. "So can we go this afternoon, Mum? Please?"

Mrs Hardwick sighed, and gave in. "All right. But we'd better go home and have some lunch first. And Mandy and James will have to ring their parents, and check that it's all right with them."

In the back of the car, Mandy and James gave each other a secret thumbs-up sign. It looked as if Ben was going to get his dog after all, even if Mrs Hardwick did seem to be regretting her decision.

"So many dogs," Ben said, his eyes wide as he stared at the row of pens filled with animals. "I wish I could take them *all* home!"

"Don't let your Mum hear you say that!" Mandy laughed.

After lunch at the Hardwicks' house, they'd all driven over to Welford Animal Sanctuary, which was just outside the village. It was run by Betty Hilder, whom Mandy and James knew well. They'd had been there many times before, but to Ben it was all new. He was so excited, he could hardly keep still as they drew up outside Betty Hilder's bungalow.

"Of course you can come and look at the dogs," Betty had said warmly as she let them in. "I've got quite a few in at the moment. Go and have a look around."

The pens where the dogs and cats were housed were in the garden behind Betty's bungalow, and Ben had hurried out there straight away, followed by Mandy and James. Meanwhile Mrs Hardwick had stopped to chat to Betty for a few minutes.

"Mandy's right," Mrs Hardwick said, as she joined the three friends. "Betty says she won't rehome animals just before Christmas, but if we find one we like, we can collect it in the New Year."

Mrs Hardwick was sounding rather gloomy again, and Mandy glanced at her nervously. Surely she wasn't going to change her mind? Not now that they were actually at the shelter, and Ben was so close to his dream of getting a dog!

Feeling rather worried, Mandy followed the others over to the row of pens. Betty had been in the middle of mucking out the stables, and she'd gone back to it, saying they could call her if they wanted extra information about any of the dogs. Mandy rather wished that Betty had stayed with them. She had a feeling that Mrs Hardwick was going to be difficult to please.

Ben was ahead of everyone else, and was already looking eagerly into the first cage.

"Oh, look at this one!" he called. "It's so sweet!"

The dog was a little terrier, not unlike Rusty, except that his coat was more sandy-coloured. As Mandy and the others gathered round, he immediately rushed over to lick Ben's fingers through the wire mesh, barking loudly.

"Oh no, Ben!" Mrs Hardwick said firmly. "He's far too noisy! I've told you, I don't want any yappy little dogs!"

"All right," Ben agreed, without looking too disappointed. "There are lots of other dogs here!"

The next cage also held a very friendly dog, a medium-sized mongrel with a shaggy black-

and-white coat. He was lying in his bed in the corner, but when he spotted Mandy and the others outside he climbed to his feet and padded over to say hello.

"He's nice and quiet," Mandy pointed out, reading the sign on the front of the cage. "And he's called Bobby. Hello, Bobby!"

"He's really friendly too," Ben remarked, scratching Bobby's head through the wire mesh.

Mrs Hardwick frowned. "He looks quite old to me. We don't want an elderly dog – it could cause all sorts of problems."

"I don't mind," Ben said wistfully.

"Your mum's probably right," Mandy said. Even if Mrs Hardwick *was* just making excuses, an elderly dog wouldn't really suit Ben. "You want a dog you can run about with."

The next dogs they saw were two lively black-and-white puppies. Ben fell in love with them instantly, and so did Mandy and James, but Mrs Hardwick wouldn't change her mind.

"No puppies, Ben!" she warned him. "That's what we agreed."

Ben nodded and sighed. Mandy felt really sorry for him. Mrs Hardwick wasn't exactly being very helpful about choosing a dog. Surely she wasn't trying to get out of it now, after she'd agreed that Ben could have a pet?

The dogs in the next row of cages weren't right either. One was a Jack Russell, which of course was too small for Mrs Hardwick; three were mongrels, whom Ben's mum said barked too much; and one was an Irish wolfhound. Mrs Hardwick almost fainted when she saw how big he was.

"It's all right, Mum," Ben grinned. "I don't think *that's* the right dog for us!"

But Mandy could see that Ben was beginning to look worried as they continued to walk up and down, looking into the cages. Mrs Hardwick was indeed proving very difficult to please, as Mandy had thought she might – or was she just making excuses on purpose because she really didn't want Ben to have a dog at all?

"I like this one." Ben stopped suddenly in front of one of the cages, and Mandy and James hurried over to have a look at the dog. Mrs Hardwick followed.

As far as Mandy could tell, this dog was perfect! She was a cross-breed, of medium size, with a short, rough white and brown coat and large brown eyes. Mandy guessed that she was probably about two years old, so she wasn't a puppy either. As Ben bent down to make friends with her, she whined and pawed at the wire mesh, but she didn't bark loudly, as so many of the other dogs had done.

"Her name's Cindy," Ben said, his eyes shining with delight. "Look, Mum, isn't she *lovely*?"

"And she seems very quiet and gentle," Mandy added quickly.

"Yes, she does," Mrs Hardwick agreed thoughtfully.

"Can we go in and see her, Mum?" Ben pleaded.

Mrs Hardwick hesitated, then nodded. "I'll go and ask Betty," she said and went off.

Ben turned to Mandy and James, his face full

of excitement. "Cindy's just perfect for me," he said happily. "I know she is!"

"She certainly looks it," Mandy agreed, stretching out a hand to tickle Cindy under the chin.

But when Mrs Hardwick came back, she didn't have Betty with her. Ben's face fell as he saw his mother coming back alone.

"Cindy must already have a new owner," he muttered sadly.

"No, Cindy hasn't found a new home yet," Mrs Hardwick explained as she joined them again. "But she's got a heart condition, so she needs an owner who can give her extra-special care."

Mandy saw Ben's bottom lip begin to tremble. "I can look after her—"

"No, Ben," his mum said firmly. "The medication and the vet's bills will be very expensive. We just couldn't afford it."

Mandy knew that Mrs Hardwick was right. It would take a very special owner to look after Cindy properly. But still, she couldn't help feeling that Mrs Hardwick was secretly relieved that she had a good excuse to turn Cindy down.

Ben was very depressed at having to leave Cindy behind, but he brightened up a little as they went on looking. He spotted two other dogs that he liked: one a mongrel with a very cheeky face, and the other a quiet but nervous-looking whippet. But, just as Mandy had suspected, Mrs Hardwick found reasons to refuse both dogs. The mongrel was too boisterous, and the other dog had been too nervous to come up to them at first, which Mrs Hardwick didn't like.

"Well, that's that then," Mrs Hardwick said as they reached the end of the last row, and Mandy was sure she could hear a note of relief in her voice. "Never mind, Ben. We'll come back again in the New Year."

"It doesn't matter," Ben muttered, his face all screwed up as if he was trying not to cry. "I'll *never* get a dog now!" And he ran off towards the car.

"Ben!" Mrs Hardwick called, but he didn't stop.

Feeling very upset herself, Mandy glanced at James. He looked as distressed as she was.

"Oh dear," Mrs Hardwick sighed. "I just wish Ben could understand . . ."

"Understand what, Mrs Hardwick?" Mandy asked quietly.

"That dogs can be more trouble than they're worth!" Mrs Hardwick burst out. "And I should know!" Then she looked worried, as if she'd said more than she'd meant to.

"What do you mean?" Mandy asked.

Mrs Hardwick hesitated. "Oh, nothing," she muttered. "It's just that I had a dog myself when I was a little girl . . ."

"You did?" Mandy was surprised.

"Yes, his name was Freddie." Mrs Hardwick's face lit up briefly. "My father gave him to me, and I loved him so much. He was a mongrel puppy when we got him, and he was very small. Tiny, in fact. But, my goodness, he grew into the most enormous dog. Nearly as big as that Irish wolfhound!"

"And what happened?" James asked.

Mrs Hardwick looked depressed again.

"Freddie was noisy and boisterous. He used to bark all the time, and he ate us out of house and home. In the end, my father insisted on giving him away." She sniffed, and Mandy saw that there were tears in her eyes. "I've never forgotten it. It was so upsetting . . ."

Mandy glanced at James. So that was why Mrs Hardwick was always going on about finding the right dog – because she'd had such a bad experience in her own childhood.

"I don't know what I'd do if Ben's dog turned out to be as bad as Freddie," Mrs Hardwick said quietly. "I wouldn't want him to be as upset as I was."

"But if you make sure you get just the right dog for you—" Mandy began.

"Well, we thought Freddie was the right dog, and look what happened!" Mrs Hardwick sighed. "If only Ben would understand that dogs are a lot of bother!" she went on. "They're just not worth it."

Oh, yes, they are, Mandy thought fiercely. It was obvious now that Mrs Hardwick didn't really *dislike* dogs. She'd loved Freddie, after all. She was just very frightened about letting another dog into her life again. And, now that Mandy knew that, she was even more determined than ever to help Ben *and* his mum find the right dog for them.

6

Success!

"Ben still seems quite miserable," James said in a low voice to Mandy, as he helped her to clear the supper things off the table, one evening the next week.

"Yes, he does," Mandy agreed, keeping a sharp ear out for Ben, who had gone upstairs to the Hopes' bathroom. "I thought he might cheer up a bit as it's getting so close to Christmas, but he hasn't."

It was now just two days before Christmas Eve. Mandy and James hadn't seen much of Ben over the last few days, as they had both been helping their families to prepare for the seasonal festivities. Mandy and her parents had been Christmas shopping over the weekend, and so had the Hunters. But, even though they'd been really busy, Mandy had kept on racking her brains for a way to help Ben and Mrs Hardwick. She still hadn't come up with anything, though. The only thing she could think of to cheer Ben up was to invite him and James over to supper to watch the next *Give a Dog a Home.* It was the last edition of the show before Christmas.

"Are you two still worrying about Ben?" Mandy's father asked sympathetically, as he began to wash up the supper dishes.

Mandy nodded. "I just know Mrs Hardwick would love having a dog again!" she said, feeling frustrated. She had told her parents about Freddie, and how nervous Ben's mum was about getting another dog. "If only she would just give it a try."

"Well, at least she's said that Ben can *have* a dog," Mandy's mum pointed out, as she finished clearing the table. "That's something."

"Yes, but I think Mrs Hardwick wants to keep putting him off, hoping he'll forget about it!" Mandy replied. "There's not much chance of that, though!"

"Ssh, Ben's coming!" James hissed as he heard footsteps on the stairs.

"Is it nearly time for *Give a Dog a Home*?" Ben asked, as he came back into the kitchen. "I don't want to miss it."

"We've still got about five minutes," Mandy reassured him.

"I wonder which dog will be on tonight," Ben said eagerly, as the three friends settled themselves on the sofa next to the Hopes' glittering Christmas tree. Mandy smiled to herself as her parents joined them. If Mrs Hardwick thought that Ben might forget all about owning a dog, she was in for a very long wait!

"Oh, great!" Ben sat up straighter as the programme started, looking more cheerful. He stared intently at the TV screen, concentrating hard, and Mandy and James grinned at each other. The Christmas tree could have fallen on top of Ben's head and he wouldn't have noticed!

"And now, on to tonight's dog who needs a good home," Fiona Ramsay went on, having given a brief rundown on what else would be on the show that evening. "A few months ago, the TLC squad received a call from an elderly man, who was very upset about his dog, a Cavalier King Charles spaniel called Buster . . ."

"I like spaniels," Ben declared.

"Cavalier King Charles spaniels are lovely dogs," Mandy's dad agreed. "They're pretty active and quite intelligent."

On-screen, the TLC squad were hurrying to a run-down-looking house in the middle of a large, industrial city. A few moments later, Andy led a chestnut-coloured dog with long, floppy ears and a thick, plumy tail out of the house, followed by Mel and Lynn.

"This is Buster," Andy said, as the camera moved to get the dog in close-up. Buster looked fairly healthy and well fed, but his coat was matted and rather dirty. "He's a year old, and we think he's basically in good health, but his owner is elderly and has arthritis, and hasn't been able to groom him regularly."

"Buster's owner isn't able to live alone anymore, and is moving in with his son." Mel took up the tale. "Unfortunately, Buster can't go too, so he's looking for a new home."

"But first he needs a bit of tender, loving care from the *Give a Dog a Home* TLC squad!" Lynn added.

The vet confirmed that there was nothing wrong with Buster that a good grooming wouldn't cure. Then, as the film switched back to Fiona Ramsay telling viewers that there would be an update later, Ben turned to Mandy and James.

"Buster would be perfect for me!" he said excitedly. "He's not too big or small, he's not too old and he's not too loud!"

"Buster does seem like a quiet, well-behaved

dog," Mandy agreed cautiously. She didn't want to raise Ben's hopes too much.

"What about your mum?" James wanted to know.

"I'll ring her and ask right away!" Ben jumped to his feet and raced out into the hall, where the Hopes' phone was. A few seconds later, he put his head round the door, looking sheepish.

"Is it OK if I use your phone, Mrs Hope?"

"Of course!" Mandy's mum laughed. "But

don't you want to wait to see the update on Buster?"

Ben shook his head. "No, I just know Buster's the dog for me!" And he disappeared again.

"He seems pretty sure!" James said with a grin.

"Well, Buster *does* seem perfect!" Mandy said slowly. "As long as Ben realises that a lot of other people are going to want him, too."

Ben was on the phone to his mother for quite a while. Mandy and James couldn't hear what he was saying as they watched the rest of *Give a Dog a Home*, but Mandy couldn't help feeling worried. What excuse would Mrs Hardwick come up with this time?

But when Ben came back into the room, he was beaming all over his face.

"Mum said yes!" he announced triumphantly.

"That's great, Ben!" Mandy exclaimed.

"Come on, let's ring right now," Ben said impatiently. "I can remember the number."

"There's no point," Mandy told him. "The

lines don't open until the end of the programme."

Ben was obviously on tenterhooks, but he sat down to watch the rest of *Give a Dog a Home*. As usual, there was an update on the featured dog at the end of the programme. After a month or two with the TLC squad, Buster's coat was now gleaming and he was glowing with health. He certainly was a beautiful dog, Mandy thought, and he seemed lively without being boisterous. Just what Ben, and Mrs Hardwick, needed!

The phone number for new owners flashed up on the bottom of the screen as usual, and Ben leaped to his feet.

"Come on, we can phone now!" he said breathlessly, and rushed out of the room into the hall. By the time Mandy and James caught up with him, Ben was already dialling the number.

"It's engaged," he said in a disappointed voice, dropping the receiver with a clatter.

"Well, lots of other people are calling too," Mandy consoled him. "Try again."

But the line was still engaged. Mandy, James and Ben took it in turns to ring, but they spent the next twenty minutes trying to get through without any success. Mandy couldn't help wondering if Mrs Hardwick had just said that Ben could ring about Buster because she had guessed that his chances of getting through weren't too good.

"I think you'd better go and use the payphone in the surgery," Mrs Hope said gently, as she came out of the living-room fifteen minutes later. "Someone may have an emergency with a sick animal and not be able to get through to us."

"Sorry, Mum," Mandy said. When the surgery was closed, emergency calls came direct to the Hopes' telephone.

"Yes, sorry, Mrs Hope," Ben added.

Mrs Hope smiled as she gave Mandy a handful of coins. "Off you go – and good luck!"

It was strange being in the surgery with no one else around, but at least it meant they weren't stopping worried pet owners from being able to contact them, Mandy thought. She picked up the phone, fed in some coins and dialled the number. But it was engaged; the same as before.

"This is hopeless!" James said in despair, after they'd spent the next half-hour trying to get through. "Everyone in England must be ringing up about Buster!"

"Maybe we should give up," Ben suggested, as Mandy took the receiver from him and pressed the "redial" button yet again.

"No, not yet," Mandy said in a weary but determined voice. Then her eyes widened in shock. "It's ringing!"

Ben and James were too stunned to say anything. Quickly Mandy handed the phone over to Ben, as a pleasant-sounding operator came on the line and said, "Welcome to the *Give a Dog a Home* switchboard. Are you inquiring about registering as a possible owner for Buster, our featured dog tonight?"

"Yes, please!" Ben said breathlessly, giving Mandy and James a thumbs-up sign.

Mandy and James gathered round Ben, listening in as the operator asked him his name, age, address and phone number, and also checked that a parent had given him permission to make the call. Then she asked Ben to explain why he thought he would be a good owner for Buster.

"She says someone will ring me about Buster before Christmas!" Ben announced triumphantly, as he put the receiver down.

"Well, you still don't know what will happen yet," Mandy pointed out gently. She didn't want Ben to get his hopes up too much. "Lots of people have rung about Buster, and only *one* person can be his new owner."

"And that will be me!" Ben said confidently. "Buster and I are perfect for each other!"

Mandy sighed, and glanced at James. She hoped that Ben wasn't going to be disappointed yet again.

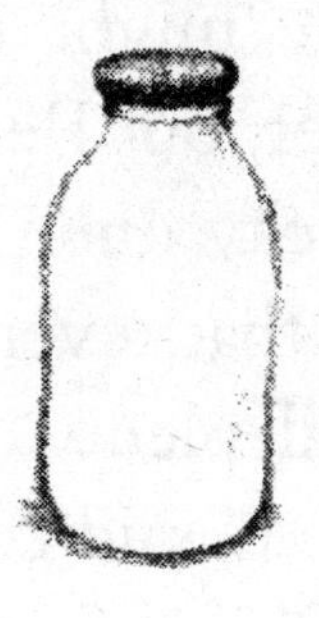

7

Mandy Has a Plan

"We'll be able to take Buster and Blackie for walks together!" Ben said happily as he held the Labrador puppy's lead tightly. "I hope they like each other!"

Neither Mandy or James replied. It was the following day, and they'd met up with Ben to take Blackie for a walk. All Ben had talked about was Buster, and how wonderful it was going to be when he finally got a dog of his own. Mandy had tried warning Ben over and over again that he might not be chosen as Buster's new owner, but Ben was sure he was going to be the lucky one.

"Just remember that, even if you don't get Buster, there are still plenty of dogs that need a good home," Mandy said carefully.

"Yes, and after Christmas the animal shelters are always looking for new owners," James

chimed in. "You'll have lots of dogs to choose from then."

Ben shook his head. "I won't need to go back to the shelter, because I'll have Buster! He's the perfect dog for me!"

Mandy sighed. Ben really had set his heart on the spaniel. She just hoped he was in with a chance.

"Mum said to come in and have a hot drink when we got back," Ben said as they reached the Hardwicks' house. Mandy and James accepted gratefully. It was the day before Christmas Eve, and the wind was bitingly cold.

"And maybe *Give a Dog a Home* will ring me this morning!" Ben looked anxious. "They said they'd call before Christmas, and that's only the day after tomorrow."

"A lot of people called about Buster," Mandy pointed out, "so it must take the kennel staff a while to go through all the details."

Mrs Hardwick was in the hall, taking off her coat, when they arrived at the front door.

"I just popped out to get a pint of milk," she explained. "It's cold, isn't it?"

"Did anyone from the programme ring, Mum?" Ben asked anxiously.

Mrs Hardwick shook her head. "Not while I've been here."

Ben glanced at the answering machine next to the telephone, and his eyes lit up. "There's a message!" he gasped, leaping forward to press the "play" button.

"Oh, it's probably your gran." Mrs Hardwick went to hang her coat up. "She said she'd ring today."

"Hello, this is the *Give a Dog a Home* switchboard—"

"It's them!" Ben yelled. "It's about Buster!"

"Ssh!" Mandy said, "We can't hear what they're saying!"

The message gave a phone number. They wanted Ben to ring them back as soon as he could. James wrote the number down, and Ben lifted the receiver with shaking fingers.

"I wonder if we'll be able to have Buster before Christmas," he said as he dialled the number. "I think I'll buy him a present just in case!"

Mandy sighed quietly. If Ben *wasn't* going to be Buster's new owner, it was best if he found out straight away.

"Hello?" Ben said breathlessly as the phone was answered at the other end. "Hello, it's about Buster . . . You left a message for me . . ."

There was silence for a moment, and then Ben's face fell. He seemed to be struggling not to cry and Mandy moved closer to him so that she could put a sympathetic hand on his arm. She glanced at Mrs Hardwick. Ben's mum looked relieved for a moment, but that quickly changed to concern because Ben was upset.

"—and so Buster will probably be rehomed with a young couple not far from his previous home." Mandy could hear what the operator was saying, now that she was standing close to Ben. "They have to be checked out more thoroughly before a final decision is made, but it looks as if Buster will have a very good home with them."

"Oh." There were tears in Ben's eyes now. "Well, thank you for letting me know—" He couldn't say any more. He quickly pushed the receiver into Mandy's hand, and his mum came over and put her arm round his shoulders.

"Thank you for taking such an interest in Buster, Ben," the operator went on, just as an idea popped into Mandy's head.

"This isn't Ben, it's his friend Mandy Hope," Mandy replied politely, wondering if Mrs Hardwick would possibly agree to her idea. "I was wondering – are the *Give a Dog a Home* kennels open to the public?"

"They certainly are," the operator told her. "The kennels are run like any normal animal shelter, except that we only have dogs here. But they're all looking for new homes."

Mandy's heart beat faster. "So do you have lots of dogs at the moment?"

"Yes, we do," the woman replied. "And we expect more in after Christmas, of course."

"Could you hold on for a moment, please?" Mandy turned to the others. "There are lots of dogs at the *Give a Dog a Home* kennels," she explained. "Maybe we could go and visit them. It would be fun to see where the programme

was filmed, even if Ben couldn't find a dog there."

"Oh, yes!" Ben said, cheering up immediately.

James grinned and nodded. "Brilliant idea, Mandy!" he said.

Mandy looked at Mrs Hardwick, who seemed in two minds.

"Aren't the kennels far away?" she asked with a frown.

"No, they're near York," Mandy replied. "I could ask my mum or dad to take us."

"Please, Mum!" Ben said eagerly. "Can we go tomorrow?"

"Tomorrow!" his mum repeated. "It's Christmas Eve tomorrow, and I've got lots to do."

Ben looked very disappointed. "But you *did* say I could have a dog, Mum!"

Mrs Hardwick looked very uncomfortable. "Well, all right then," she agreed reluctantly.

Mandy gave a sigh of relief, and spoke to the operator again. "Can I have the address of the kennels, please?"

As she wrote it down, Mandy secretly hoped that her plan would work. She wanted to cheer Ben up, but that wasn't the only reason why she had suggested a visit to the *Give a Dog a Home* kennels. Mrs Hardwick might start finding reasons to reject all the dogs she saw yet again, but this time she would have Andy, Mel and Lynn to deal with. And, if anyone could find the right dog to suit Mrs Hardwick, it was the TLC squad!

8

Full Steam Ahead!

"You want me to drive up to the *Give a Dog a Home* kennels tomorrow?" Adam Hope put down his newspaper and stared at Mandy and James.

"Well, only if you can, Dad," Mandy said hopefully. "Mrs Hardwick would probably take us, but she might find some excuse!"

"I suppose this is all about finding a dog for Ben?" Mandy's father said with a smile. "There are lots of other local animal shelters you can try, you know, without rushing off to York!"

"I know," Mandy agreed. "But I really want to see the kennels where the programme's made."

"I wouldn't mind seeing them myself, as it happens," Adam Hope said thoughtfully.

"And York isn't that far away, Dad," Mandy went on.

"True," Mr Hope agreed.

"And I just know that the TLC squad will be able to find a dog that Mrs Hardwick likes!" Mandy finished eagerly.

Her dad grinned. "Oh, you're going to bring in the big guns, are you? Well, let's see if the famous TLC squad will be able to help!"

"Does that mean you'll take us, then?" Mandy asked.

"All right, you're on," Mr Hope agreed. "But we'll have to leave early. The roads will be very busy with people going Christmas shopping and visiting relatives or whatever."

Mandy and James cheered.

"But only if your mum thinks she can cope with the surgery on her own tomorrow," Mr Hope added quickly.

"Of course I can," Mandy's mum agreed, coming into the room and overhearing the end of the conversation. "We don't have many appointments booked in at the moment."

"That's great!" Mandy said, giving her mum a hug and beaming at James. If all went to plan tomorrow, Ben would at least know he was getting a dog soon, even if it didn't arrive in time for Christmas . . .

"Morning, Mandy."

Gran was coming up the path of Animal Ark as Mandy opened the front door. It was the following day, and Mandy, James and Mr Hope were leaving bright and early for the journey to the *Give a Dog a Home* kennels in York. They were picking Ben and his mum up on the way.

"Hi, Gran." Mandy gave her a hug. "What are you doing here?"

"I'm going to do some last-minute Christmas shopping, and I wondered if your mum wanted anything," Gran told her.

"How's Grandad?" Mandy wanted to know.

"He's fine, except that he's convinced it's going to snow!" Gran replied. "He was out in the garden yesterday evening, covering up all the tender plants."

"It *does* look like snow," James said, squinting up at the grey-coloured sky.

"A white Christmas!" Mandy exclaimed. "That would be brilliant!" Ben and his quest

for a dog had taken up so much of her time since school had finished, Mandy had hardly had time to think about Christmas at all. But now she was beginning to feel excited. There was only one day to go! And if they could find Ben his dog today, Christmas would be utterly perfect.

"Come on, you two. We'd best be off." Adam Hope came out of Animal Ark, buttoning up his coat. "I want to try and beat the traffic if possible. Oh, hello, Mum."

"Where are you all off to?" Mandy's gran wanted to know.

"To the *Give a Dog a Home* kennels," Mandy replied. "We're going to find a dog for Ben."

"Yes, and one that Mrs Hardwick will like!" James added.

Gran smiled. "Get the TLC squad to sort it out, then," she advised, and Mandy grinned.

"That's exactly what we're going to do, Gran!" she said as she climbed into the Land-rover.

As they pulled up outside the Hardwicks'

house, Mandy could see Ben's face at the window, watching for them eagerly. A moment later, he came rushing out of the front door, followed by his mum.

"The weather forecast on the TV said it's going to snow today," Mrs Hardwick said anxiously, as she climbed into the passenger seat next to Adam Hope. "Maybe we shouldn't be going."

Ben's face fell, and Mandy couldn't help feeling rather annoyed. Mrs Hardwick was *always* making excuses where dogs were concerned!

"Well, it's not a long journey to York," Mandy's father reassured her, "and if the weather turns bad, we can easily head for home again."

Mandy crossed her fingers for luck inside her warm red gloves. *Please, don't let it snow until we've got back home*, she willed silently.

"I hope you find a dog today, Ben," James said in a low voice. Mandy's dad and Mrs Hardwick were discussing the weather, and weren't listening to them.

Ben sighed. "Even if I do, Mum will probably think of some reason why I can't have it."

Mandy smiled to herself. Ben didn't know that she intended to enlist the help of the TLC squad to deal with Mrs Hardwick's objections!

"Let's just wait and see, shall we?" she said.

In the front seat, Mrs Hardwick had begun telling Mandy's father about her childhood dog, Freddie. Mandy, James and Ben listened in silence as she explained how upset she'd been when Freddie had to be given away.

"That's a shame," Mr Hope commented, when Mrs Hardwick had finished the story.

"Yes, and that's why I keep telling Ben how important it is to get the *right* dog for us," Mrs Hardwick said firmly.

"True," Mr Hope agreed. "But it's also just as important that the *dog* gets the right home, too."

Mrs Hardwick was surprised. "What do you mean?"

"Well, although you loved Freddie, he wasn't the right dog for you," Mandy's dad went on.

"He was too big for your house, and too noisy. But you weren't the right owners for Freddie, either. He needed somewhere with more space, and it sounds like he got bored. That's why he barked so much."

"I never thought of that." Mrs Hardwick sounded shocked. "I know that my father gave him to some people who lived on a farm in the countryside, and they thought he was a wonderful dog. Of course, Freddie would have had lots of space to run about, and plenty to do on a farm."

"The dog has to be right for the owner, and the owner has to be right for the dog," Adam Hope said gently. "It has to work both ways."

Mrs Hardwick was silent for a long time after that. Mandy wondered what she was thinking. Maybe now she would see that it was no one's fault that Freddie hadn't fitted into her family, and hopefully she wouldn't be quite so worried about letting Ben choose a dog.

As they drove the last few kilometres towards York, Mandy, James and Ben were on the lookout for the first sign to the *Give a Dog a*

Home kennels. It was in the countryside, just outside the city.

"There it is! There it is!" Mandy and Ben called out together, as Mr Hope joined the long queue of traffic leading up to a large roundabout.

"And we're only three kilometres away," James added.

As the Land-rover finally turned into the kennels car park, Mandy felt her tummy turn over with excitement. There was the familiar entrance where Fiona Ramsay stood every week to introduce the beginning of the programme. The TLC squad's red van was parked in one of the spaces, but there weren't many other cars about.

"I think we picked a good day to visit," Mandy's dad remarked, as they all climbed out of the Land-rover. "Most people will be out finishing their Christmas shopping."

"I should be able to get a good look at all the dogs, then!" Ben said eagerly.

Mandy glanced at Mrs Hardwick. She still looked a little nervous, but not as worried as she had been when they went to the local animal sanctuary. Mandy began to feel a bit more hopeful.

They all went through the main entrance and into the kennels' reception area.

"It's a lot smaller than it looks on TV, isn't it?" James whispered to Mandy and Ben, as they all went over to the reception desk.

"I wonder if the TV crew are filming here today," Ben said eagerly.

Mandy was longing to see if any of the TLC squad were manning the desk, but she was disappointed. The receptionist, a small, plump woman with glasses and brown hair, was very nice, though, and explained that they could wander around and look at the dogs on their own. And if there was one they liked the look of, they would be able to go in with a kennel-hand and get a closer look.

"Are the TV people filming here today?" Ben asked.

The receptionist shook her head. "No, the current series was filmed a while ago. They'll be filming a new series sometime after Christmas."

As everyone else went over to the entrance to the kennels, Mandy lingered at the reception desk.

"Are the TLC squad here this morning, please?" she asked in a low voice.

"Yes, they're around somewhere," the receptionist replied, with a twinkle in her eye. "Even though they're TV stars now, they still have to help with cleaning out the kennels! But if you want their autographs, just ask!"

"Thank you," Mandy said, and ran to catch

the others up. It would be nice to get the TLC squad's autographs, but that wasn't the most important thing. Most of all she wanted them to convince Mrs Hardwick that somewhere in the kennels was the perfect dog for Ben, and for her!

9

A Bit of TLC

"Oh, Ben, I don't think that dog will do at all!" Mrs Hardwick held up her hands in horror. "He's far too noisy, and look how dirty he is! He obviously enjoys rolling in the mud!"

Mandy sighed. The dog they were looking at was a handsome black-and-white Border collie, but he was certainly not the pet for Mrs Hardwick.

So far they had walked round half of the large kennels, and they hadn't yet found a dog that Ben and his mum could agree on. Mrs Hardwick was obviously trying hard to be more open-minded, but she still seemed very nervous that they might make the wrong decision. She examined every dog that they saw carefully, before deciding that something or other was wrong with it. Mandy longed to say that dogs were just like humans – people weren't perfect, either! But she thought that might sound a bit rude, so she kept quiet.

There was no sign of any of the TLC squad, which was also worrying Mandy. How could she ask them to help, if they were nowhere to be seen?

"Look at this one!" Ben had stopped in front of the last kennel in the row, and was staring in. A fluffy white dog, which looked as if it might be part poodle, trotted over to the front of the cage to say hello.

"She's cute!" Ben said, pushing his fingers

through the wire mesh to scratch the dog's head. "What do you think, Mum?"

"Oh, Ben, not a white dog!" Mrs Hardwick exclaimed. "Think how dirty it would get!"

James looked at Mandy and shrugged his shoulders, while Mr Hope raised his eyebrows.

"This is hopeless!" James whispered to Mandy. "Mrs Hardwick is *never* going to give in!"

Mandy thought that James was probably right. Even the talk Mandy's father had had with Mrs Hardwick during the journey hadn't done the trick. As everyone else moved on to the next row of kennels, Mandy lingered behind to stroke the little white dog.

"Sorry," she murmured as the dog looked up at her with big, brown eyes, "but I don't think even a Crufts Supreme Champion would please Mrs Hardwick!"

As Mandy hurried on to catch up with the others, she suddenly heard a soft little bark. Puzzled, she stopped and looked around. It sounded very close, and she wasn't that near to any of the kennels. Then she noticed she was standing next to a small shed. There was one at the end of each row of kennels, but Mandy had no idea what they were for. Then she heard it again, the same soft little bark.

The window was quite high, but Mandy grabbed hold of the ledge, and hauled herself up. Unfortunately the glass was quite misted on the inside and she couldn't see very much. But as Mandy stared in she could just make out a shaggy chestnut-coloured body, and a tail wagging like crazy. There was a dog in there!

"Can I help you?" said a voice from behind her.

Mandy was so surprised, she let go of the window ledge and crashed to the ground. She was even more surprised when she looked round to see Andy, Mel and Lynn, holding buckets and brooms and smiling at her. It was the TLC squad.

"Are you all right?" Mel asked, hurrying forward to Mandy. "Sorry we startled you."

"I'm fine!" Mandy gasped. She stared at Andy, Mel and Lynn as if she couldn't quite believe that they were real. It was very strange to meet someone you'd only seen on TV, Mandy thought. But the TLC squad seemed just as friendly and down-to-earth as they did on the programme.

"Are you looking for a dog?" Lynn asked with interest.

"No – I mean yes!" Mandy tried to get her breath back. "Well, my friend, Ben, is, but his mum doesn't like any of them. I wondered if you could help."

"You'd better tell us the whole story," Andy said gently.

Quickly Mandy told the TLC squad exactly what had happened. "And I think Mrs Hardwick would really love to have a dog," Mandy ended up. "But she's just so scared that Ben will choose one that isn't right for them."

"I see." Andy grinned at Mandy, then nodded at Lynn and Mel. "Well, I think you might have already solved this problem on your own, Mandy, without our help!"

"What do you mean?" Mandy asked, puzzled.

But before Andy could say anything else, Ben, Mrs Hardwick, Mr Hope and James came hurrying back to look for Mandy.

"There you are," Ben exclaimed. "We thought you'd got lost." Then his jaw dropped. "It's the TLC squad!" he stammered.

"At your service!" said Andy, giving a sweeping bow.

"Wow!" gasped James, shoving his glasses up his nose so he could get a better look. "It really is you!"

"Which one of you is Ben?" Lynn asked.

"I am," Ben said immediately.

"We hear you're looking for a pet," Mel said. "Would you like to tell us exactly what kind of dog you're hoping to find?"

"Well . . ." Ben glanced sideways at his mum. "I just want a dog I can play with and take for walks, but Mum doesn't want a noisy dog, and she doesn't want one that's too big or too small. It can't be white either, because it will get too dirty. And she doesn't want a puppy, or an old dog. Oh, and it mustn't have anything wrong with it."

Mrs Hardwick turned red and gave an embarrassed smile. "Oh dear. You must think I'm very fussy!" she muttered.

"Not at all," Lynn reassured her. "It's much better to know exactly what sort of dog you *do* want."

"And why do you think a dog would like to come and live with you?" Mel asked Ben's mum. Mandy grinned as Mrs Hardwick's mouth fell open. She obviously hadn't expected that!

"Well – er—" Mrs Hardwick faltered. "We've got a nice house and quite a big garden. And I'm at home in the daytime, so the dog wouldn't be left on its own."

"That's good," said Andy approvingly. "So you're looking for a quiet, well-behaved dog, who's perhaps had some basic training?"

"Well, yes." Mrs Hardwick nodded, as Mandy and James glanced at each other and smiled. The TLC squad was really putting Mrs Hardwick on the spot!

"Problem solved!" Lynn beamed. "Mandy's already found the perfect dog for you!"

"I have?" Mandy gasped.

"You have?" Ben cried.

"Yes, come this way!" said Andy, leading everyone over to the little building Mandy had been looking into. "This is one of the temporary sheds where we house the new arrivals while we prepare their kennels."

Mandy's eyes opened wide as she remembered the chestnut-coloured dog she had caught a glimpse of inside the shed.

"Sasha only came in this morning," Andy went on, as he unlocked the door. "She's a Cavalier King Charles Spaniel."

"Just like Buster!" Ben's face lit up.

"She's only two years old, but she's had some basic training and she's very quiet and well-behaved for such a young dog." Andy pushed open the door, and smiled at Mandy, Ben and James. "Why don't you go in and say hello?"

Her heart beating fast, Mandy followed James and Ben into the shed. There, waiting for them and wagging her tail, was one of the most adorable dogs Mandy had ever seen. Her coat was silky and well groomed, and her eyes were bright and intelligent.

"Oh, she's perfect!" Mandy gasped.

"She's a lovely dog," James added. But Ben was speechless; all he could do was stand and stare.

"Come on, Ben!" Mandy encouraged him gently as Sasha, eager to be stroked, padded over to them on her shaggy paws. "Say hello to her."

Ben knelt down, and Sasha rubbed her head on his knee. She was obviously a very friendly dog, without being at all boisterous and unruly.

"She's just what I want!" Ben said in a choked voice.

The TLC squad, Mr Hope and Mrs Hardwick were watching from the doorway, as the shed wasn't really big enough for them all to cram inside. Mandy looked at Ben's mum to see her reaction. She was staring down at Ben and Sasha, who was sitting quietly, allowing them all to stroke her and enjoying every minute of it.

"I'm a vet, so do you mind if I have a quick

look at her?" Adam Hope asked the TLC squad.

"Not at all," Andy said. "Our own vet hasn't examined her yet, so we'd be interested to know what you think."

Mandy watched with her heart in her mouth as her father gave Sasha a quick examination. If there was anything wrong, her dad would say so, even if it meant Ben wouldn't be able to have the spaniel. Ben was looking very nervous indeed, and Mandy gave him a reassuring smile. From what she could see, Sasha looked in the best of health, but the final word was down to her father.

"She's certainly got a lovely personality," Adam Hope remarked, as he finally released the spaniel. "She put up with me examining her without a murmur – I wish all my patients were like that!"

"What do you think, Dad?" Mandy asked urgently.

"She's in excellent condition," Mr Hope said, and Mandy, Ben and James all sighed with relief. "She's obviously been well-looked after."

"She belonged to a young couple who've gone travelling the world for a couple of years," Mel explained. "They hated parting with her, but they just didn't have any relatives or friends who could look after her for that length of time."

"So what do you think?" Lynn asked, and the three members of the TLC squad turned to look intently at Mrs Hardwick.

Ben's mum turned pink. "Well—" she began, then stopped.

Everyone waited to hear what Mrs Hardwick had to say. Mandy's heart began to race and she crossed her fingers firmly behind her back. What would Ben's mum decide?

10

And a Happy New Year!

"Well—" said Mrs Hardwick again. At the moment she didn't seem able to say anything else.

As Mandy looked at Mrs Hardwick staring down at Sasha, she suddenly had a brainwave.

"Go on, Sasha!" she whispered, giving the

dog a gentle push towards Ben's mum. "It's now or never!"

Obediently, Sasha trotted across the shed towards Mrs Hardwick. She stopped at her feet, and waited politely for Ben's mum to reach down and pet her.

"Goodness me, she *is* very well-behaved, isn't she?" Mrs Hardwick said in amazement. "I hate those dogs that jump up at your legs."

As if she was agreeing with her, Sasha gave a soft little bark and gently licked Mrs Hardwick's fingers.

"She likes you, Mum!" Ben pointed out happily.

Everyone waited in silence as Mrs Hardwick continued to fuss Sasha. Mandy could see that Ben's mum was smiling, and she kept her fingers crossed. If ever there was a dog who could melt Mrs Hardwick's heart, it had to be this beautiful little spaniel.

"I think Sasha's already decided who her new owners are going to be!" Mel said with a grin. "But it's up to you, of course!"

Ben stared at his mum with a pleading look

on his face. "Can Sasha be our dog, Mum? Please?"

Mrs Hardwick looked at her son, and then down into Sasha's trusting brown eyes. "I think we've found the perfect dog for us at last, Ben," she said with a shaky smile.

"Oh, thanks, Mum!" Ben gasped with delight, and hurled himself across the shed to give Mrs Hardwick a big hug. Meanwhile Sasha's tail wagged madly from side to side,

and Mandy and James glanced at each other in delight. Ben had got his dog at last, and she was a beauty!

"Congratulations." Andy shook hands with Ben and his mother. "You couldn't have chosen a better dog!"

"I won't be able to take her home for Christmas though, will I?" Ben asked, picking Sasha up and hugging her. The spaniel didn't mind at all, and lay quietly and contentedly in her new owner's arms.

Mandy felt so pleased, she could almost burst. It had been worth all the trouble they had gone to, just to see the thrilled look on Ben's face.

"I'm afraid not," Mel told him. "You'll have to wait till the New Year, and there'll also have to be a home check."

"But we don't live in York!" Ben said, suddenly looking rather worried.

"That's OK," Andy reassured him. "Because of the programme, our new owners come from all over the country. If we can't get to you, we usually ask your local animal shelter to do the home check and report back to us."

"I wish I didn't have to leave you here over Christmas, Sasha," Ben whispered in the spaniel's silky ear. "But I'll buy you lots of presents, and you can have them later."

"Just a minute, Ben." Lynn had slipped away from the shed a few minutes before. Now she had returned with a Polaroid camera in her hand. "If you like, we can take your picture with Sasha, so that you've got a reminder of her until she comes to live with you."

"Yes, please." Ben flushed with pleasure, as everyone moved out of the way so that Lynn could get a good shot of him and the spaniel. "But I want you to be in the photo as well, Mandy," Ben went on. "If it wasn't for you, I'd never have found my perfect dog!"

Mandy blushed, and went to stand next to Ben.

"Right, look this way!" Lynn called as she looked through the lens, and they did as she said – even Sasha. The picture slid out of the camera and, after it had developed, Lynn handed it to Ben.

"I'll pin this up in my bedroom as soon as I get home," Ben said proudly. "Doesn't Sasha look cute, Mandy?"

"She's gorgeous," Mandy agreed.

"Look!" James gasped, pointing at the window. "It's snowing!"

Mandy glanced outside. Sure enough, large white snowflakes were floating slowly down to the ground.

"It's snowing, and I've got a dog!" Ben said happily as he carefully put Sasha down. "This is going to be the best Christmas ever."

"Thank you very much," Mandy said to the TLC squad, and Ben nodded.

"Not at all." Andy shrugged. "*You* were the one who found Sasha, Mandy."

"Let us know how Sasha gets on, won't you?" Mel said.

"And keep watching *Give a Dog a Home!*" Lynn added.

Mrs Hardwick looked at Mandy and James. "Thank you for all your help," she said with a smile. "And you too, Mr Hope."

Mandy grinned at Ben as the spaniel padded

over to them for one last goodbye cuddle. She couldn't have asked for a better Christmas present than seeing Ben's joyful face as he stroked his new dog.

"Bye, Sasha," Ben said, fondling the spaniel's silky coat. "I'll see you again very soon."

"Bye, Sasha," Mandy whispered. "And Merry Christmas!"